The Little Red Hen

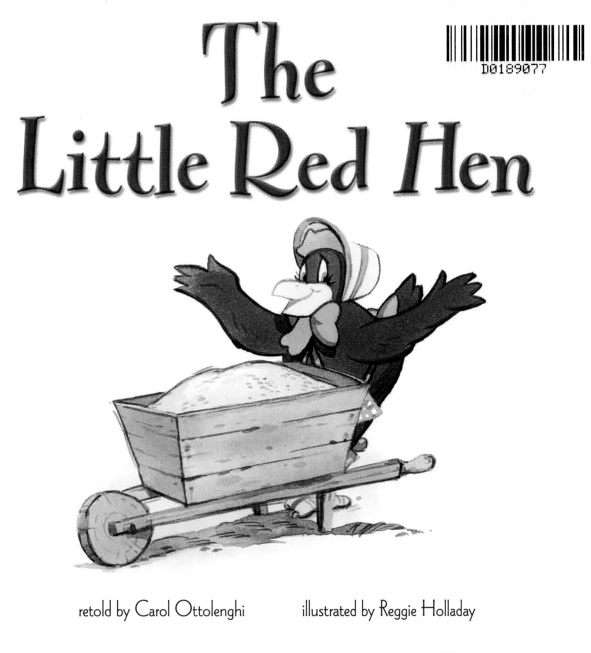

retold by Carol Ottolenghi   illustrated by Reggie Holladay

nce upon a time, a Little Red Hen lived on a farm with a dog, a pig and a cow. The Little Red Hen grew flowers to make into special teas. The dog, the pig and the cow lazed about in the warm sun. They ate and slept and watched the Little Red Hen work in her garden.

The Little Red Hen scratched the ground every morning, looking for her breakfast. One day she dug up some grains of wheat.

"Look!" she squawked to the other animals. "If we plant this grain, we'll have bread with our tea."

"Who will help me plant the grain?" asked the Little Red Hen.

"Not I," said the dog. "I'm gnawing this bone."

"Not I," said the pig. "I'm stirring the mud."

"Not I," said the cow. "I'm swatting flies with my tail."

The Little Red Hen sighed a little sigh. "I guess I'll have to plant it myself," she said.

And she did.

All summer long the Little Red Hen watered and weeded her wheat. But the dog, the pig and the cow always said they were too busy to help.

By the end of the summer, the wheat stood tall and golden. It was ready to be cut and threshed.

"Who will help me cut and thresh the wheat?" the Little Red Hen asked the other animals.

"Not I," said the dog. "It's naptime."

"Not I," said the pig. "There are new apples to eat in the orchard."

"Not I," said the cow. "I'm chewing my cud."

The Little Red Hen sighed a big sigh. "I guess I'll have to thresh it myself," she said.

And she did.

She cut the wheat with her sharp beak. Then she tied it into bundles and shook loose all the grains.

The Little Red Hen loaded the wheat grains into a wheelbarrow. *It would be nice to have some help pushing this to the mill,* she thought.

"Who will help me take the grain to the mill?" the Little Red Hen asked the other animals.

"Not I," said the dog. "I have to guard the farm."

"Not I," said the pig. "I can't walk that far."

"Not I," said the cow. "I would get lost."

The Little Red Hen humphed a little humph. "I guess I'll have to take it myself," she said.

And she did.

At the mill, the miller poured the grain between the millstones. The stones turned round and round, grinding the grain into soft, powdery flour.

The road back to the farm was dusty, and the wheelbarrow was heavy. But the Little Red Hen forgot her tired wings every time she imagined how scrumptious her fresh-baked bread would taste.

When she got back to the farm, she asked the other animals, "Who will help me bake some bread?"

"Not I," said the dog. "I don't know how to cook."

"Not I," said the pig. "I have to curl my tail."

"Not I," said the cow. "I'm too big for the kitchen."

The Little Red Hen humphed a big humph. "I guess I'll have to bake it myself," she said.

And she did.

The Little Red Hen made bread dough by mixing the flour with some salt, water and yeast. After the dough rose, she put it in the oven to bake. Soon a warm, fragrant smell filled the farmyard.

The Little Red Hen pulled the loaf out of the oven. The outside of the bread was crusty and golden brown. The Little Red Hen knew the inside would be white and chewy and delicious.

"Who will help me eat the bread?" the Little Red Hen asked the other animals.

"I will," said the dog. "Watching the farm is hungry work."

"I will," said the pig. "That wonderful smell makes my mouth water."

"I will," said the cow. "I'm finished with my nap."

The Little Red Hen shook her head. "No you won't," she said.

"Why not?" asked the other animals.

"You would not help me plant the grain," said the Little Red Hen. "You would not help me cut and thresh the wheat. You would not help me take the wheat to the miller. You would not help me bake the bread.

"So you are not going to help me eat the bread, either. I will eat the bread myself."

And with a nice cup of tea, she did!